Lizzy

The Lonely Zebra

C.M. Harris

Ashlynn Feather

The Lonely Zebra
by C.M. Harris

All rights reserved.
Published by Purple Diamond Press 2021
Text & Illustration Copyright © 2021 by C.M. Harris
Villa Park, CA

Illustrated by Ashlynn Feather
Edited by Elena Marinaccio

This is a work of fiction
No part of this publication may be used, reproduced, stored in a retrieval system, or transmitted in any form whatsoever or by any means, electronic, mechanical, photocopying, recording or otherwise, without the prior written permission from both the copyright owner and publisher.

Paperback: ISBN: 978-173553725-2
Hardcover: ISBN: 978-173315243-3

Library of Congress Control Number: 2020916315

Purple Diamond Press
PO Box 5357, Orange, CA 92863

Printed in China

Visit www.CMHarrisBooks.com for more information
This book can be purchased directly from the author.
Special discount for large quantities for schools/organizations.
info@PurpleDiamondPress.com

The Lonely Zebra

Standing Up and Using Your Voice to Help Others

Embrace the beautiful differences that make you who you are!

"C'mon, let's go," **Zola** giggled. "Do you want to play hide-and-seek?"

"I do, I do!" Said **Zach**.

Zola and Zach are best friends, two little Zebras who love to play and laugh all day.

Today is Zach's last day playing in the plains as he and his family are moving far, far away.

"I'm hot. I need water," said Zola. "Zach, I'm going to the watering hole. I'm thirsty."

Zach quickly stopped running.

"No, Zola, wait! Hank is there!" Zach said. "We can't play at the watering hole. He's too mean to you, and that's not how I want us to spend our last day together."

"Aw, okay," Zola whimpered.

And off they ran to find somewhere else to play.

Hank, the hyena, is **not nice**, not very nice at all. He moved to the plains not too long ago. Whenever he sees Zola he laughs and says unkind things about her, just because Zola has a special spot of missing stripes.

The next day Zola went out to play in the grasslands but was all alone.

Zach moved far away and she now has no one to play with. This made Zola very **sad**.

Zola sat on the ground playing in the dirt when she thought she heard laughter.

She peeked behind the rocks nearby.

She could see the other animals: **Hank** (*hee-hee-hee*) the hyena laughing with **Gene** the giraffe, **Malik** the meerkat, and **Carl** the crocodile;

Laini the leopard hopping in circles with **Hana** the hippo;

Grant the gorilla chasing **Chad** the Cheetah with **Leo** the lion,

and **Raina** the Rhino dancing with her two best friends **Olivia** the ostrich, and beautiful **Edna** the elephant.

Zola wished she could play and they could all be friends again but she was too scared to say hello. She wished with all her might that Zach would come back to play, but her wish hadn't come true. Zola decided to head home and find something else to do.

On her way back home Zola thought about all the fun she used to have playing with Grant, Edna, Chad, and the others.

"Why does Hank have to be so **mean** to me? I wish he was nicer."

Zola slowly trotted on home with her head down low and her hooves dragging along the ground.

"Ouch!" Zola was not paying attention to where she was going and bumped into Sara. "Oh, I'm sorry, I didn't see you there." Zola apologized.

"It's okay, I forgive you" **Sara** cheerfully said. "I'm new here and was looking for someone to play with!" Zola grinned from ear to ear, "I'll play with you!"

Sara was a beautiful black Swan, a very special Swan and heard Zola's wish, but which wish can Sara make come true?

Sara and Zola spent the afternoon playing, dancing, and singing.

"It's getting really hot, I need to go for a swim." Sara said.

"There is a big watering hole." Zola shared.

"Yay! Let's go take a dip!" Sara yelled in excitement, but Zola started to **worry**, she didn't want her new friend to see Hank laugh at her.

"Well I don't really go there," said Zola.

"Why?" Asked Sara.

"There's a hyena that likes to laugh at me." Zola shyly said.

"But don't all hyenas laugh?" Asked Sara.

"I guess so, but Hank says mean things about my stripes." Zola sadly said.

"I **love** your stripes, who cares what Hank thinks! When I was teased, my mommy told me something I never forgot…"

Sara remembered hugging her mommy and said,

" '**Sometimes others might say hurtful words to you because someone else said hurtful words to them, but that doesn't make it right**.'

We can't let Hank hurt you, even though he's mean to you we can still be nice to him. C'mon, let's go take a dip in the water. Let's be brave!"

Zola thought Sara was right! But she was still scared to go to the watering hole. When they got there all the animals were laying out in the sun and telling jokes.

Zola tried to hide behind Sara.

"Hi, there! I'm Sara, I'm new here." She said.

Sara and Zola sat on the ground next to each other.

As soon as Zola laid down, there was Hank. "(hee-hee-hee) Zola... (hee-hee-hee) you can't sit..."

But just as Hank was going to finish saying something Sara waved her wings in front of Zola to protect her from Hank.

"Oh no you don't, if you are not going to say something nice then don't say anything at all !"

Hank froze, no one had ever stood up to him before. Zola and the others were surprised that Sara was so brave. Edna, Malik, Gene, Raina, and Carl all looked at each other.

"Hey, there's plenty of space here for all of us," Grant said. "We can all hang out together."

Zola saw the **sadness** in Hank's eyes.

Zola smiled at him, "Hank don't be sad, we can all play and have fun together. I forgive you for making me feel sad."

"(hee-hee-hee) Really? But I wasn't very nice to you," said Hank.

"I know but a special friend told me that we can still be nice to others, even when they're unkind to us." smiled Zola.

"I'm **sorry** Zola. I'm sorry for being mean to you, I..I..I was jealous of your pretty stripes."

Zola's eyes filled with tears as she felt so **happy** he said sorry, she gave Hank a big hug. Hank's apology made everyone feel better.

Sara and all the others spent the rest of the day having so much fun together.

Before the sun set everyone said good-bye, with great big smiles on their faces, and headed home.

Zola and Sara walked home together.

"Thank you Sara!" Zola hugged her and smiled.

"Don't mind Hank, I don't think he'll bother you anymore, and hey, what are friends for? I'm glad I could help." Said Sara.

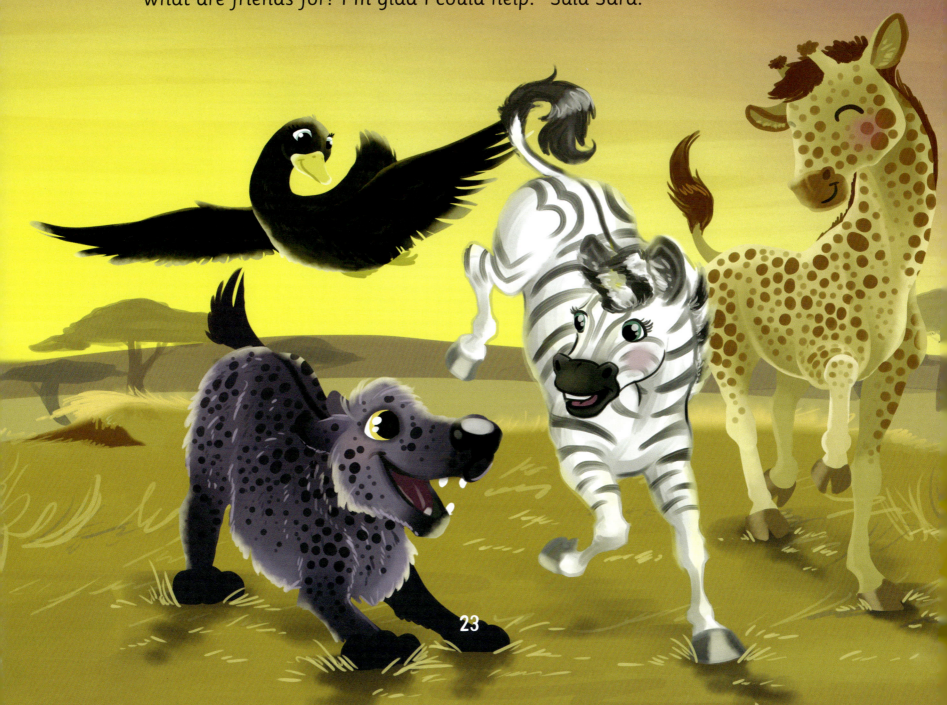

Zola went inside to tell her mom all about her fun day and off Sara flew, awaiting to help her next new **friend.**

About The Author

Charity Michelle Harris, award-winning author of **What If We Were All The Same!** spent her childhood worrying what other kids thought about her. She was teased for being skinny and for the way she walked, due to being diagnosed with Charcot Marie-Tooth Disease at the age of seven. Charity wrote **The Lonely Zebra** as a reminder to children that not only is it important to be kind to others but that we can also forgive and be friends with people who were unkind to us.

Charity lives in Southern California and enjoys visiting schools where she spreads the importance of friendship, acceptance, and inclusion. Charity loves working with children and was a private tutor for over ten years.

To read more about Charity's journey, visit **www.CMHarrisBooks.com**.
The author can be contacted by email at books@cmharrisbooks.com

May you be so kind and write an Amazon review, every review is appreciated and helps very much.

@CMHarrisBooks

@CMH_Books

Kindness Challenge

Have you ever felt like Zola, the lonely zebra?

Being left out and not feeling included is not a fun feeling and can cause some people to feel sad and alone. It's important for everyone to be included.

Did you notice anything about Zola on the book cover?
She is **TEAL**! Teal is a beautiful color that is known to represent open mindedness, free of judgment, and embracing differences. Zola had a special friend, Sara the swan who helped the other animals be kind and show that we too can forgive those who hurt us and be friends again.

Can you show Zola and Sara how you can **BE KIND**?

We challenge you to be kind to someone you know or even someone you don't! It could be a simple hello or a big sorry.

Today, I will be kind by

_____

Did you spot what made Zola's stripes **DIFFERENT**?